D0016126

WHO GIVES A HOOT?

BY **JACQUELINE KELLY**

WITH ILLUSTRATIONS BY **JENNIFER L. MEYER**

HENRY HOLT AND COMPANY · NEW YORK

HENRY HOLT AND COMPANY, *Publishers since 1866*
Henry Holt® is a registered trademark of Macmillan Publishing Group, LLC
175 Fifth Avenue, New York, NY 10010
mackids.com

Library of Congress Cataloging-in-Publication Data

Names: Kelly, Jacqueline, author. | Meyer, Jennifer L., illustrator.
Title: Who gives a hoot? : Calpurnia Tate, girl vet / by Jacqueline Kelly ;
with illustrations by Jennifer L. Meyer.
Description: First edition. | New York : Henry Holt and Company, 2017. |
Series: Calpurnia Tate, girl vet | Summary: Calpurnia and her grandfather
rescue a barn owl from the river and, with the help of Dr. Pritzker, dead
mice, and some detective work, nurse it back to health.
Identifiers: LCCN 2017023455 (print) | LCCN 2016050876 (ebook) | ISBN
9781627798747 (Ebook) | ISBN 9781627798730 (hardcover) | ISBN
9781250143396 (paperback)
Subjects: CYAC: Veterinarians—Fiction. | Naturalists—Fiction. | Barn
owl—Fiction. | Owls—Fiction. | Family life—Texas—Fiction. |
Texas—History—1846-1950—Fiction.
Classification: LCC PZ7.K296184 (print) | LCC PZ7.K296184 Who 2017 (ebook) |
DDC [Fic]—dc23
LC record available at https://lccn.loc.gov/2017023455

Our books may be purchased in bulk for promotional, educational,
or business use. Please contact your local bookseller or the Macmillan
Corporate and Premium Sales Department at (800) 221-7945 ext. 5442
or by e-mail at MacmillanSpecialMarkets@macmillan.com.

First edition, 2017 / Designed by April Ward
Printed in the United States of America by
LSC Communications, Harrisonburg, Virginia
1 3 5 7 9 10 8 6 4 2

For animal lovers everywhere

MICE MOVE OUT
25¢ PER BOX
R.U. OLEANDER

CHAPTER 1

1¢ WILL BUY

BEST CANDLE BOXES

"Calpurnia," Granddaddy called up from the bottom of the stairs, "are you ready? The barometer predicts a fine day for us."

"Yessir! Coming!" I knew we could count on the barometer on the library wall; it was never wrong. I grabbed my butterfly net and ran downstairs at top speed. It was October 1, 1901, and we were going to spend the day floating down the San Marcos River in our boat. Now, "boat" makes it sound rather grand, but it was really only a leaky old rowboat barely big enough for the two of us and our gear. This was fine with me, as I didn't want any of my six brothers coming with us. Can you imagine being the only girl right in the middle of six brothers? Ugh, the burdens I have to bear.

Anyway, I called our vessel the *Beagle* in honor of the ship Mr. Darwin sailed in. For five years, he traveled around the world collecting fossils and bottled beasts and dried flowers from far-off lands. Granddaddy was the captain of our *Beagle*, which was only fitting, as he was older than me and had also been a captain during the War Between the States. His job as captain was to row, although he'd let me row if I wanted to. (Let me tell you, it's harder than it looks. The first time I tried it, I flipped straight over on my back like a click beetle.)

I was the first mate. My job was to scoop out the water that kept seeping into the bottom of the boat, threatening our equipment and our boots. This "bilgewater" kept me busy. I also took notes in my Scientific Notebook of the plants and animals—flora and fauna— we discussed on the way. One of the nicest things about a rowboat is that you sit facing each other, which makes it easy to talk.

Even though our vessel wasn't much to look at, and even though my bailing tool was only a rusty bucket, and even though the quiet river we floated along wasn't much more than a stream, I always felt we were setting off in a grand barque with three tall masts and yards of flapping sails, plunging through the white-tipped waves, the salt spray in our faces. And every one of our "voyages" was a grand adventure to parts unknown. Never mind that we had to turn around at the second bridge to make it home in time for dinner.

We untied our boat and set off. A few inches of mist hung above the water so that we seemed to be rowing through the clouds. Every now and then, a fish jumped and made a faint splash.

"Where shall we sail today, Calpurnia?"

I thought about it and said, "How about the Canary Islands? Or maybe Patagonia? What about Tasmania?"

"All fine destinations," he said, pulling on the oars. "I'll let you decide."

I was mulling it over, when suddenly a small, silvery fish leaped from the water and landed in the bottom of our boat.

"Look!" I said. I'd never seen this happen before, and I stared at the fish in surprise. It appeared to be a small perch or fountain darter. I grabbed at it, but twice it wriggled from my grasp. I got it on the third try and flipped it over the side, where it quickly swam away.

Granddaddy said, "Perhaps we should choose South America today. It was there that Darwin first saw flying fish. They do not actually fly by flapping their fins, but jump from the

water at high speed and glide above it to escape predators. They can stay in the air for half a minute and travel amazing distances, several hundred yards at a time. It's quite a sight, especially when a whole school of them launch themselves at once."

"Then let's go to South America today in honor of our own flying fish," I said.

Granddaddy rowed, the oars creaked, and in between taking notes, I bailed water and imagined a whole bunch of flying fish skimming their way down the river, more like a flock of birds than a school of fish. That would be something.

Granddaddy hummed some Mozart, which he did when he was happy. It was a piece my piano teacher, Miss Brown, had forced me to learn, so I chimed in from time to time. We sounded quite good together. But then a mockingbird burst into joyful song and put our paltry human efforts to shame.

"Ah," said Granddaddy, "the *Mimus polyglottos*, or 'many-tongued mimic.' How lucky we are to have it sing us on our way."

The mockingbird lived up to its name by first running through imitations of the robin and blue jay and owl. Then it launched into songs of its own, wild and exuberant. If you've never heard a mockingbird, I hope you'll be lucky enough to hear one soon. It will mimic anything and everything—barking dogs, ringing bells, creaking doors—mix it all together in a new song, and sing the results as loud as it can.

As he rowed, Granddaddy pointed out some likely spots for hunting fossils. We'd had a heavy rain three days before, which had washed away parts of the riverbank, thus exposing treasures that had remained hidden for millions of years. Sometimes we'd also find arrowheads left behind by the bloodthirsty Comanche who had hunted here for centuries before being driven onto the reservation in the Oklahoma Territory.

Granddaddy pointed at the bank and said, "There's a new area of exposed sedimentary rock. That looks promising."

We beached the *Beagle* and set to work on the outcropping, Granddaddy gently tapping with a small hammer while I brushed away the chips and dust with a soft brush. He stopped after a few minutes and pointed at the rock.

"Look," he said, "do you see that?"

I looked but could see nothing special. "Uh, no."

"Take the hammer and this chisel. Tap here first, and then here, but not too hard. You want to try to get it out intact."

I still didn't know what "it" was, but I followed his instructions, chipping away and doing my best to be careful.

Slowly, a shape emerged—a rounded piece of rock.

"Can you tell what it is yet?" said Granddaddy.

I stared at it. The rock looked coiled and ribbed. "Oh, I think it's an ammonite!"

I'd been hoping to find one of my own to match the one in Granddaddy's collection. His was the size of a dinner

plate. This one looked smaller, about the size of a saucer, but just as nice and detailed.

I worked away, slowly freeing the once-living creature from the rock, while Granddaddy told me about ammonites, a kind of mollusk that had lived in the ocean millions of years ago.

"It looks like the nautilus shell in the library," I said.

"Indeed. The nautilus is the ammonite's closest living relative, followed by the clam and the oyster."

An hour and a half later, I ran my fingers over the perfect spiral. I held in my hand an extinct animal that had once lived at the bottom of a former ocean, and now on dry land on which I stood. The animal had died in the water and been trapped in mud that slowly turned to rock. The rock had kept it hidden for millions of years until I, Calpurnia Virginia Tate of Fentress, Texas, freed it. I held my newest treasure aloft in the sun, thinking, *Water . . . rock . . . air . . . light.*

"Yes," said Granddaddy, nodding. He seemed to understand perfectly. I had a sudden picture in my mind of how he must have looked as a young boy, holding his first fossil up to catch the light.

He smiled and said, "Even though that shell is now a rock, it is still breakable. Wrap it up carefully to protect it until we get home."

I wrapped my find in old newspapers. He explained that the missing soft parts of the ammonite probably looked like those of a squid, and that it captured prey with its tentacles and ate it with a beak that looked like a parrot's. I would have to find a special place on my shelf of precious treasures to display it, perhaps next to the hummingbird's nest.

By then it was lunchtime, so we sat down to eat our sandwiches. Granddaddy talked about two men in western Colorado who were digging up huge fossils of ancient "thunder lizards" or "dinosaurs." Professor Cope and Professor Marsh were bitter rivals, racing to dig up the biggest and most complete dinosaurs to send to the museums in the big cities back East. Some of their finds were bigger than a horse, and some were bigger than a house. Some flew like birds, and some swam in the ocean. Some lived alone, and some hunted in packs. Some ate plants, and some ate other dinosaurs. There was something special about the soil in that area that was good for preserving bones and then heaving them to the surface. I wondered how you could dig out something that size, and how you'd display it. If I found something like that, I'd have to put it in the barn where my little brother Travis kept his ever-changing zoo.

"Perhaps we could go to Colorado one day," I said. "Perhaps we could take the train. After all, it's only a couple of states away. I wonder if I could talk Mother into it. You'd have to help me. You'd have to tell her it was for educational purposes."

Granddaddy smiled. "I don't believe that's the kind of education your mother has in mind for you."

"You're right." Scrambling through the dirt and digging up ancient dead things was my idea of a good time but not hers. There was no understanding it. I said, "We might have to think of something else."

"Your grandmother once had family in that area."

I perked up at this. Perhaps Mother might let me go after all.

"I haven't spoken with them in many years," he said.

"Why not?"

"They sided with the North during the War, and they asked me to join them. Of course, I knew it was a useless conflict from the start, but I felt it my duty to put on the uniform of my homeland, the South. They never spoke to me again. All my letters were returned unopened."

"But the War was over a long time ago," I said, doing some arithmetic in my head. "Thirty-six years ago, to be exact. *And* it's a whole new century. How can they still be mad?"

"To some people it is never over."

"Well, we're talking about dinosaurs, not the War. Do you think we could go to Colorado? Mother would never let me go on my own in a million years, so we'd have to go together. I bet if you asked her she'd say yes." But even as I said this, I had my doubts. Nobody in our family had ever made such a trip, *especially* not to dig up what she'd no doubt call a bunch of old bones. We'd have to tell her we were "visiting family." That's the kind of thing she'd like.

"Will you write to them, Grand-daddy?" I pleaded. "We should at least try, don't you think?"

"All right. I'll see what I can do."

I kissed him on the cheek.

"Now," he said, "if you'll excuse me, I'm going to have a short rest." He pulled his knapsack under his head and tilted his hat down over his eyes. "Kindly wake me in half an hour."

"Yessir." I did not have a watch, but he'd taught me to tell time by the movement of the sun in the sky.

I tried to nap as well, but the mockingbird was making quite the racket. I found myself thinking of dinosaurs. Did they shake the ground when they walked? How fast could they run? If you took a time machine back

23

to their era, would they be able to run you down and eat you? How long did they live? Would they make good pets? Not the meat-eating ones—those sounded like a nightmare—but the plant-eaters. Travis, who was crazy about all animals, would probably want one as a pet. I could just see him trying to stuff a giant brontosaurus into our barn, the long tail sticking out one side and the long neck sticking out the other, happily munching on hay while my brother patted the leathery hide and asked him if he was a good boy.

And people in town called *me* the crazy one. Ha! If they only knew.

S oon it was time to wake Granddaddy, and we set out again. I
bailed for a while and wondered if
Father would be willing to have the
Beagle fixed and made watertight. The
sun shone, the mockingbird mocked,
and my grandfather gave a fascinating
talk about the difference between newts

and skinks and salamanders. I took notes as he talked. He knew everything about everything, and I loved him for it. I hoped that one day I would know everything about everything too.

The rest of the trip was quiet, right up to the swimming hole near Zapata's farm. We were gliding along. We were minding our own business. There was not a reason in the world to think our lives were about to change. Nope, no reason at all.

A sudden blur of movement caught the corner of my eye, followed by a sudden splash. Was it a little fish jumping to escape a bigger fish? Was it some rotten boy throwing rocks at us? Who would dare? I turned to look and saw, to my shock, an owl in the water.

What went through my head was this: (1) why, that's an owl, (2) and it's in the water, (3) but owls don't belong

in the water, (4) therefore it can't be an owl, (5) but it *is* an owl, (6) and it's in the water, (7) but owls don't belong—

I might have sat there thinking in a circle all day like an idiot if Granddaddy hadn't snapped me out of it by saying, "Calpurnia, your net, if you please."

"Oh, right." I scrambled for my butterfly net as the owl thrashed its wings. I wouldn't exactly call it swimming, but it was managing to move slowly away from us. Granddaddy turned the boat and made a strange call that sounded sort of like this: *deek deek deek*. The owl stopped splashing for a moment and turned its white heart-shaped face to stare at us with coal-black eyes. Not liking what it saw—two humans instead of another owl—it thrashed harder and struck out for the other shore. We caught up to it without too much trouble, owls not really being aquatic types, as you probably know.

I stood up to snag it with my net, and we wobbled and tipped alarmingly. (Rowboats are very good for rowing in but very bad for standing in.)

"Careful now," said Granddaddy while I fought for my balance. I was just about to pitch over the side, when Granddaddy leaned the other way, righting the boat and saving me from going into the drink. I could just see the headlines in the local newspaper:

GIRL NATURALIST DROWNS OWL WHILE TRYING TO SAVE IT. TRAGIC MISTAKE. CLOTHES RUINED, MOTHER FURIOUS. LAUGHED AT BY ALL.

"Thanks," I puffed. "I think I can reach it."

I stretched with my butterfly net and swished it through the water. The owl saw it coming and ducked away. I swished again, and it ducked away again. Its feathers were now getting waterlogged, and it was starting to sink. I figured I only had one more chance. This time I swished at it from behind so it didn't see the net coming. I managed to snag the poor creature just as it was going under.

"Got it!" It screeched and thrashed and sprayed water everywhere, but it

was surprisingly light, and I lifted it out of the water without any trouble. It lay snarled in the net at the bottom of the boat, flapping and making a terrible racket. You'd think it would be grateful, but it only looked fierce and angry. I thought it very beautiful.

Granddaddy said, "It is a barn owl, or *Tyto alba*, quite young from the look of it."

"What's wrong with it? What was it doing in the water?"

"The answer will have to wait until we can get it home for a proper examination. Or perhaps not. Look up ahead—there's Dr. Pritzker on the bridge."

I tore my eyes away from the owl, and sure enough, there was Dr. Pritzker waving at us. I waved back. I liked Dr. Pritzker. He was our town's only animal doctor. (The proper word for this is *veterinarian*.) He was usually so busy it was rare to see him out for a stroll.

"Ahoy!" he called. "What have you got there?"

Granddaddy said, "It's a barn owl we pulled from the river. It's hurt in some way."

"Well, bring it ashore, and let's take a look."

This surprised me because Dr. Pritzker didn't normally tend to wild creatures. He had his hands full with cattle and horses and other such valuable farm animals. But he and

Granddaddy were friends; I figured that's why he agreed.

By now the owl was exhausted and lay still, blinking in the bright light.

CHAPTER 3

MICE
MOVE OUT

25¢
PER BOX

R.U. OLEANDER

1¢ WILL BUY

BEST
CANDLE
BOXES

We docked, and I got out carrying the owl in my arms, still in the net. Granddaddy and Dr. Pritzker shook hands. They had met when the doctor had moved to town after losing his home and practice in the terrible storm in Galveston a few months before. To save himself from the rising waters, he'd climbed into a tall oak tree. But the tree turned out to be swarming with rattlesnakes who'd all had the same idea, and he'd been bitten on his right arm. The hand had withered, and now he shook hands with his left. He often required help with tasks that needed two good hands. I helped him out around the office making labels for medicines, and sometimes he'd let me trail along behind him when he made farm calls. We were lucky that he'd decided to start life anew in Fentress.

"Well, Captain Tate," the doctor said, "you're certainly carrying unusual cargo today." For a moment, I thought he meant me.

"Indeed," Granddaddy said. "It's good of you to examine it for us."

"I'm happy to, but I can't promise much. Birds are not my normal patients. Hello, Calpurnia. I'd shake your hand, but I see you have your arms full."

The owl was dripping all over me. I didn't mind. (Mother would have minded, but then, she wasn't there, so it didn't matter, right? I figured I'd be mostly dry by the time we got home.)

He went on, "Let's leave it in the net until we get to my office. Do you need any help?"

"No, thank you, I can manage. It hardly weighs anything."

"That's because birds have hollow bones, a special adaptation for flight," said Granddaddy.

I carried our patient the short distance to Dr. Pritzker's office. It lay still in my arms, probably scared half to death, and glared at me. Somewhere during the rescue, it had managed to rip a hole in my butterfly net, and I wasn't too happy about that, so I glared back at it. I'd have to save my allowance

Dr. Pritzker

for a new net. (I found out later that owls always glare, even when they're happy. It's just the way their faces are made; you can't take it personally.)

We followed Dr. Pritzker into his office, and I put the owl on the exam table. It started to thrash again and screamed at the top of its lungs.

Have you ever heard a barn owl scream? At the top of its lungs? At close range? I'm not sure I can describe it but I'll try: Think of, oh, say, a million cats fighting in a sack; think of a witch being boiled alive—no, make that a dozen witches; think of . . . well, it's like nothing else on earth.

Dr. Pritzker threw a small towel over its head, and it fell silent.

Whew.

We uncovered our ringing ears, and Dr. Pritzker said, "How did you find it?"

"It fell into the river, and we fished it out," I said.

"But owls don't just drop on you from the sky."

"This one did," I said.

"Indeed, it remains a mystery," said Granddaddy, "a mystery that we hope you can solve for us."

He held the owl while Dr. Pritzker unfolded one of the wings and gently stretched it out to its full length. The wing was cream and gold colored, with spots and bars of brown scattered over it. For having such a small, light body, the bird had surprisingly large wings.

Granddaddy said to me, "Look, Calpurnia. Notice the very fine fluff along the leading edge of the wing. This muffles the noise as it flaps its wings. It is the only bird we know of that can fly silently. You see, it has to in order to catch mice, which have very good hearing."

I thought about the birds in our lives—pigeons, herons, chickens—and realized that every one of them made some kind of noise while flying.

"Hmm," said Dr. Pritzker, "this wing looks fine. No feathers missing. I don't see any blood." He gently ran his good hand along the bones of the wing. "Nothing broken here. Now let's look at the other one."

The towel slipped, and the owl

snapped at Dr. Pritzker's good hand, making a loud *tchikk*. Granddaddy quickly put the cloth back in place before the bird could shred one of the doctor's remaining healthy fingers.

"That was close," Dr. Pritzker said. "If I injure my good hand, I'll be out of business."

"You don't need to worry, Dr. Pritzker," I said. "I'll be your partner. We can do it together."

He smiled one of those smiles that grown-ups smile when they're not taking you seriously. Why would he do that? He'd told me several times what a

good helper I was. Now, if only I could get him to convince Mother . . .

Granddaddy said, "Farmers find these owls useful because they control mice and snakes. They must catch four or five mice every day merely to survive. They hunt by their acute sense of hearing. It is said they can hear a mouse's heart beating under a foot of snow."

"Really? Gosh." I tried to imagine this kind of sensitivity. I doubted I could hear a mouse's heartbeat even if I stuffed it all the way down my ear hole. (And even though I had done many

48

strange things for Science, this was—
even for me—pretty unlikely.)

Dr. Pritzker examined the claws
before slipping off the towel and taking
a look at the big black eyes.

Dr. Pritzker inspected the other
wing and said, "I can't find anything
wrong with it."

We stared at the owl. The owl glared
back. It was slowly drying off.

"Do you think it's hungry?" I said.

Dr. Pritzker ran his hand over the
bird's stomach and said, "It hasn't
eaten for a while."

"We brought our lunch with us;

maybe it would eat some of that." I opened one of our knapsacks and pulled out what was left of my sandwich. "Do you think this will do? It's ham and cheese."

I handed Dr. Pritzker a hunk of sandwich. He placed it near the owl's foot. Nothing. It paid the ham and cheese no attention at all.

"I think," said Granddaddy, "that we will have better luck with its native food, namely, a mouse. Doctor, do you by any chance happen to have any mice about you?"

Dr. Pritzker laughed and said, "I

just might. Calpurnia, will you please check the mousetraps in the storeroom and see if there's anything in there for this fine fellow to eat?"

The storeroom contained, among other things, sacks of grain, always appealing to the common house mouse, *Mus musculus*, along with his country cousins. Dr. Pritzker always kept traps baited with cheese in all four corners of the room. Sure enough, an unfortunate victim lay dead in one of the

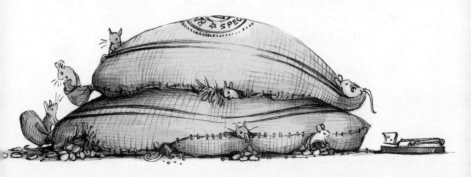

traps; unable to resist the cheese, it had paid for it with its life. I picked it up by the tail, trap and all, and took it back. Granddaddy was telling the doctor about the many species of owls in Texas and how they were classified.

"Ah," Granddaddy said, "let us see if we can tempt our new friend's appetite."

Now, mouse for lunch is not my idea of a treat, but then, the owl probably felt the same way about my sandwich.

"We'll need to take it out of the trap," said Dr. Pritzker.

Granddaddy was holding the owl,

and Dr. Pritzker couldn't do it one-handed. Which left me. Oh, good. I put the trap/mouse on the table and pulled up the spring bar to release the body. Which was kind of awful. Buck up, Calpurnia, I told myself, it's all for Science. You can do this. And *don't* look squeamish about it. You can't look squeamish when you're trying to be taken seriously. (Good thing my sensitive younger brother Travis wasn't there. Travis loved all animals, especially cute little furry ones. Plus he tended to faint at the worst moments.)

I think I did a pretty good job of not

looking squeamish. The limp body lay on the table in front of the owl, which ignored it.

"Come on, bird," said Dr. Pritzker, "time for you to eat."

It showed no interest at all.

"We need a piece of string," said Granddaddy, "between two and three feet long."

String? What for? We both stared at him for a moment. But since Granddaddy knew everything there was to know about Nature, Dr. Pritzker did not question him. He fetched a ball of twine and scissors, and I cut it to the right length.

"Tie it loosely to the mouse. Not too tight."

I followed his instructions and made a loop around the mouse's hind paws.

"Now," said Granddaddy, "pull the mouse across the table, and stand back as far as you can."

Uh-oh. You really needed to pay attention when Granddaddy told you to stand back from something. He didn't kid around about such things.

I stood back and pulled on the string. The mouse slid across the table. Faster than we could blink, the owl spread its wings, jumped a foot in the air, and pounced on the mouse and

ripped it loose from the string and flipped it upside down and swallowed it whole. Headfirst. It was all over before we knew what had happened.

MICE MOVE OUT

25¢ PER BOX

R.U. OLEANDER

CHAPTER

4

1¢ WILL BUY

BEST CANDLE BOXES

"Gosh!" I said.

"Good heavens," said Dr. Pritzker.

"Yes, the predatory instinct is impressive," said Granddaddy. "Think of the owl as a machine built by Nature to hunt mice—moving mice, that is. Its hunting instinct is triggered by a small animal moving quickly. This instinct exists in larger animals as well, and that is why one should never run from a bear or vicious dog—it will pursue you."

We could see the bulge of the mouse moving down the esophagus to the stomach. Not a pretty sight. (I was *really* glad Travis wasn't there. He'd have keeled over on the spot. It's handy he turns a pale greenish color before he flops over; it's usually enough of a warning for me to catch him before he hits the ground.)

Granddaddy went on, "The owl digests the mouse's flesh, but it cannot digest the fur or tail or skeleton. It will bring the skeleton back up in a few hours encased in a pellet."

"Bring them back up . . . as in . . . ?" I said.

"Regurgitate, yes."

"Oh."

"The pellets make for interesting study, containing, as they do, the mouse's skeleton."

"Ah."

"I'm sure you'll have a fascinating time dissecting it."

"Ah. Yes. I'm sure I will."

"Our new friend looks like it will be with us for a while, so we better think about a cage and a jess."

"What's a jess?" I said.

"It's a leather ribbon you tie around the owl's foot to use as a leash. People who hunt with falcons and hawks use them to control the birds. And you'll need a stout leather glove and a cage to keep it in, of course, until it heals from whatever is ailing it."

"So you think it will live?" I asked Dr. Pritzker.

"Well, it certainly has an appetite, and I can't find anything obviously wrong, so those are both good signs. If it refused food, I'd be a lot more worried about it. But I won't be able to keep it here," he said, looking at me. "It's going to need good nursing care and regular feedings, and it will be important to keep the cage clean."

Now Granddaddy was looking at me as well.

"Oh. Okay," I said.

And just like that I was elected the owl wrangler. Which I supposed would be quite interesting except for the part about feeding it five mice per day. Every single day.

How would we get it home? And

then I remembered Polly the Parrot, who lived across the street at my father's cotton gin. Polly was a huge bird who usually spent his time walking back and forth on a perch in the manager's

office, where he regularly alarmed visitors with his own sudden shrieks and hooked beak and sharp black claws. Polly had a carry cage that was seldom used, and I felt sure it would fit our new patient.

I ran across the street to the gin to borrow it, leaving the doctor and Granddaddy deep in a discussion of bird anatomy.

Luckily, the assistant manager, Mr. O'Flanagan, was in his office. He said he'd be happy to lend me the cage after I explained the situation. Polly paced back and forth on his perch and

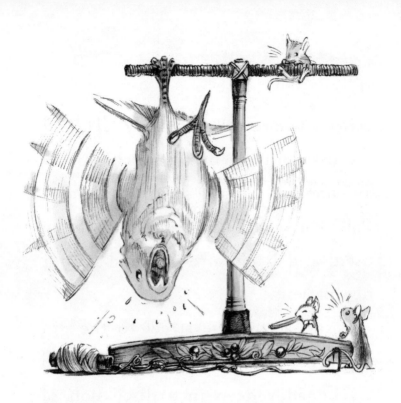

muttered quietly to himself like a crazy bird. Then, without warning, he erupted in one of his earsplitting screeches that always made Mr. O'Flanagan burst into laughter, and made me want to run for my life. And even though he was really, really loud, for the first time in his whole life Polly no longer held the title of The Loudest and Most Annoying Bird in Texas. That owl had him beat by a long shot, I'm telling you.

I carried the cage back to Dr. Pritzker's office. The doctor was busy wrapping a leather strap around the owl's lower leg while Granddaddy held the bird and kept the towel in place. Dr. Pritzker's clawed hand looked a lot like the owl's foot.

"There we go," he said, standing back and inspecting his handiwork.

"That'll do for now. And look, Calpurnia, I've found a leather gauntlet." He held up a stout leather glove that went halfway up the arm. "Can't remember why I got this, but it's perfect. Put it on."

"Me? Uh, okay."

The glove was far too big for me, but it protected my hand, which was the important thing.

Granddaddy said, "Now, take the jess between your fingers and don't let go. Let the bird perch on your hand. Keep your arm straight to keep it away from your face."

Uh-oh. I took hold of the jess, and
he slipped the cloth off the bird's head.
The owl screeched and tried to launch
itself into the air, flapping its wings
like mad but going nowhere, the wind

from its wings buffeting my face. Then, a few seconds later, it quit flapping and perched quietly on my wrist, pretty as you please. It looked like it had been sitting there its whole life.

"Well, now," said Dr. Pritzker, "that makes quite a picture."

"Indeed," said Granddaddy. "It's a shame we don't have a photographer here in town to capture the two of you: GIRL WITH OWL."

While they admired us, I was busy worrying about the thickness of the leather versus the strength of those claws. But nothing happened, and we managed to slip the owl into Polly's cage, where it sat quietly, swiveling its head in all directions. It actually looked quite at home. Maybe it just needed a mouse inside it to calm down.

"There now," said Granddaddy. "Shall we row it home, or would you rather walk?"

It wasn't all that far to walk, but the cage was awkward. Dr. Pritzker volunteered to drive me home in his wagon. Granddaddy went back to the *Beagle*, and I helped Mr. Pritzker harness his buckskin mare, Penny. We clip-clopped home at a gentle pace so as not to disturb our passenger.

My brothers Travis and Sul Ross were playing catch on the front lawn as we rolled up.

They gaped at the owl and ran over to see it, babbling so many questions I didn't know which one to answer first. The owl stepped nervously to the far end of the perch, trailing the jess.

"Calm down," I said to my brothers. "You're scaring it."

I waved good-bye to Dr. Pritzker and told my brothers how we'd found the owl. Then Travis said, "What are you going to do with it?"

This stopped me in my tracks. "I don't know. I hope it gets better soon so we can release it."

"Can't we keep it? I've already thought of a good name for it."

"No, no," I said hastily. Granddaddy always said you should never name wild animals. It's the first step in getting too attached to them to let them go. "No names."

"But it's a good one."

"No!"

"Let's call it Ollie the Owl."

"No, Travis."

"Don't you like it? I think it suits him."

"It might be a her for all we know, but that doesn't matter. No names!"

A few minutes later, we had Ollie the Owl in the back corner of the barn, where it was darkest. (He looked quite at home there, which I guess was only natural for a barn owl.)

"Do you think he'd let me pet him?" said Travis.

"That's a terrible idea," I said. "Don't even think of it."

"She's right, young man," said Granddaddy behind us, and we both jumped. He'd made it home and joined us in the barn without making a sound. "Do not try to pet it. You could lose a finger or an eye. Now, if you'll excuse me, I have to catch up on some reading. And do keep an eye out for the pellet; it should make for interesting study."

He left us as quietly as he'd arrived.

"What's the pellet?" said Travis. "What's he talking about?"

"Never mind," I said.

Travis eventually wandered off to tend to Bunny, his big, prizewinning fluffy rabbit, leaving Ollie and me to blink at each other. A few minutes later, the owl leaned on one foot and then the other, twitched its head, opened its beak wide, and horked up a large, dark mass.

Now, I don't know about you, but to me the word *pellet* suggests something small and dry and tidy, right? But not so. The pellet was a vaguely mouse-shaped wad of wet fur and bones at the bottom of the cage. Ack. It was one of the more disgusting things I'd ever seen, and, believe me, I've seen a whole lot of disgusting things in my time. But

I told myself that it
was for a good cause.
And doing Science makes
you tough. I didn't want to end up
all tenderhearted and lily-livered like
Travis, fainting at the sight of blood
and guts and the least little thing.

Honestly,

what could you

do with a boy like that?

    Anyway, rather than put my hand in

there with that beak and those claws, I found a stick and dragged the wet pellet to the side of the cage close enough to reach it through the bars. I picked it up. Still warm. And squishy. Gaaah.

Travis came back and said, "What's that?"

I said, "It's probably better that you don't look. The owl threw up what's left of its lunch."

"You mean Ollie? He did?" said Travis, backing away. "So that's owl vomit?"

"Yep."

"Why?" He turned pale. That's what he usually did before turning green.

"It's just what they do. You see, they—"

"See you later," he said, and took off.

"Travis, wait! I need your help. We've got to find some mice. Dead or alive, it doesn't matter."

No answer.

"Hey!"

Too late. He was gone. I was on my own with this one.

We had our own mouse-control system, which consisted of two parts: the inside part and the outside part. Inside, we had Idabelle the Inside Cat, who patrolled the kitchen and the pantry,

and slept in her own basket by the stove. Our cook, Viola, doted on her. Outside, we had mousetraps and Alberto, the hired man, who was in charge of baiting and emptying the traps.

I went to him and said, "Uh, Alberto, you empty the mousetraps, right?"

He looked at me. "*Sí*, Miss Calpurnia."

"So, uh, could you save me the mice?"

"*¿Qué?*"

"The mice. The dead mice. From when you empty the traps."

"You want me to give you the *ratón muerto*? The dead mouse? This is what you mean?"

"Yes, please. As many as you can."

He frowned and said, "What for you want the dead mouses?"

"I need them for, uh, an experiment."

"Is okay with your mama?"

Here we approached dangerous ground. Mother would pitch a fit if she knew I was collecting dead mice for any reason whatsoever, even for such a worthy project as saving an owl's life. I sidestepped the question by saying, "Grandfather Tate and I need them for a project." I hoped that using Granddaddy's name would smooth things over.

He thought for a moment. "For Señor Tate is okay. I give you the dead mouses."

The next morning, I found a small sack in the barn with five dead mice in it. Lovely. And so I spent my time wiggling a dead mouse on a string while staying out of reach of those claws and

that beak. Not an easy task, I'm telling
you, but Ollie ate them all. Even though
I visited him several times a day, it
was hard to get too attached to him.
He was beautiful, but he was wild and

dangerous. And even though I knew better than to compare his behavior with that of a human being, let's not forget he had the world's most disgusting table manners.

CHAPTER 6

MICE MOVE OUT.
25¢ PER BOX
R.U. OLEANDER

1¢ WILL BUY

BEST CANDLE BOXES

So what was wrong with Ollie? None of us could figure it out. The answer finally came from the unlikeliest place: the Fentress General Store.

Mother, who was constantly mending my brothers' shirts, had sent me to the store for a spool of white thread. I waited my turn at the counter behind Mr. Holloway, who was counting out his money for a box of candles and chatting with the owner, Mr. Chadwick.

Mr. Chadwick took the money and handed Mr. Holloway his change.

"Oh, wait," said Mr. Holloway. "You got any of that newfangled mouse poison? I've heard it works pretty good."

Mr. Chadwick reached under the counter and pulled out a red box with a skull and crossbones on it. "This is what you're looking for. They eat it up,

and then they run off to die. But you've
got to keep this stuff away from kids
and dogs and cats."

"How much?" said Mr. Holloway.

"Twenty-five cents a box. I know it's

kind of expensive, but then you don't have to buy any more traps, so that's a savings right there. And look, it says right here on the box: 'guaranteed mouse poison, fast and effective.'"

Mr. Holloway grunted and nodded. He fished in his pocket for a quarter and plunked it down on the counter.

Up until that moment, I'd been daydreaming of various dinosaurs roaming the streets of our town. But then the word *mouse* seeped into my brain. Followed by the word *poison.* Then a voice in my head said, *Wake up, nitwit, you need to hear this.* Since it seemed important, I woke up and paid attention. I tugged on Mr. Holloway's sleeve.

"Yes, missy?"

"Mr. Holloway, you're going to poison mice?"

"Yep. They're pretty bad this year. There used to be an owl about, but now he's gone. Moved on to some other barn, I expect. Why do you ask?"

I thought, *Because a poisoned mouse leads to a poisoned owl. And a poisoned owl will fall from the sky without a mark on it. And if it's very lucky, it will land in the river. And if it's very, very lucky, a girl and her grandfather will be rowing by just in time to fish it out.*

I had done it . . . I thought. I had solved the riddle of the owl that fell from the sky. "I'm pretty sure I know what happened to the owl," I said. "He got ill from eating a poisoned mouse. We've been feeding him mice out of traps to make him stronger, and you can have him back in a few days. But you won't be able to use that stuff; it might kill him."

"Well," he said slowly, scratching his beard, "I'd rather have the owl, truth be told. He don't cost me nothin'." He broke into a wheezy laugh.

The box had a lot of tiny writing on it. I needed a closer look at it. I needed to show it to Dr. Pritzker and Granddaddy.

"Mr. Chadwick," I said to the storekeeper, "can I borrow that box for a day? I won't use it. And I promise I'll bring it back in tomorrow."

Mr. Chadwick was reluctant to lend it to me but said he'd sell it to me. He'd charge it to our family account but then erase it once I brought it back unopened and in good condition the next day. That seemed fair enough. He wrapped it up in brown paper, and I took off running with it at full speed. I practically had wings on my feet, I was that excited.

I made it home in record time, clutching my package. I ran through the front door and was just about to knock on the door to the library, where Granddaddy spent most of his time, when Mother called out from the parlor across the hall.

"Goodness, Calpurnia, what took you so long? I've been waiting for my thread."

Ugh! I'd completely forgotten.

I made another trip, running both ways. A long, exhausting half hour later, I knocked on the library door, panting and puffing.

"Enter if you must," called Granddaddy.

I went in and shut the door behind me. He took one look at me and said, "Are you all right?"

"Yes, Granddaddy. I brought you something. I think it explains why the owl fell in the river."

He unwrapped the parcel and smiled. "Yes, I think you're right. Smart girl."

I blushed red-hot under his praise.

He took his magnifying glass out

of the desk drawer and inspected the tiny writing. "Hmmm. There are instructions for an antidote here. Let us visit Dr. Pritzker and see what he has to say about it."

"Shall I bring Ollie?"

"Ollie?"

"That's the owl. I'm not the one who named him," I added hastily. "Travis did."

"Ah, yes."

I borrowed my younger brothers' little red wagon, and we put Ollie's cage into it, bumping down the road with Ollie blinking and grumbling in the light. We got some funny looks on

94

the way, I can tell you, but then the two of us often did. I was used to it; I don't think Granddaddy even noticed.

Dr. Pritzker had just returned from a farm call and was unpacking his bag when we arrived. He looked a bit worried when he saw we had Ollie with us and said, "How's the patient? Something wrong?"

"Not at all. In fact he's getting fitter every day," said Granddaddy, "and it appears that Calpurnia has arrived at a diagnosis."

"Really? How's that?"

I showed him the box and told him

what I'd heard at the store. I could tell at first he didn't believe me. But then he started smiling, and the more I talked, the bigger he smiled.

"I think you're onto something," he said. "Let's go inside and take a look."

We put Ollie's cage on the exam table, and Dr. Pritzker pulled out his own magnifying glass and peered through it at the box.

"'Antidote,' it says here. 'In case of accidental poisoning, combine one tablespoon of charcoal with one tablespoon of bicarbonate . . .'" He read to the bottom and looked up.

"Ha! I have everything we need right here. The only problem is going to be getting him to swallow it."

So how do you get medicine into an owl? Why, the same way you get poison into him. You stuff the medicine into a dead mouse, of course. What could be easier?

"I'll check the storeroom," I said.

Fortunately, one of the traps held a dead mouse. Dr. Pritzker measured and poured the antidote, then took a tiny spoon and pushed as much of it as he could down the mouse's gullet.

"Will you do the honors, Calpurnia?" said the doctor. "After all, it's your patient and you made the diagnosis."

For once, feeding Ollie felt exciting and not like some terrible chore. I tied a length of string to the mouse, put it in front of him, and tugged.

And do you know what happened? Why, absolutely nothing. For the first time in his life, Ollie did not pounce on a moving mouse. The only mouse in the whole world he really needed to eat, and he would not do it. He yawned and stretched his wings. I could have killed him.

I tugged on the mouse again. He preened his feathers. But I caught a glint in his eyes.

"What's *wrong* with him?" I wanted him to get better so we could release him into the wild and I'd never have to do mouse duty again.

"Try again," said Granddaddy.

I put the mouse on the far side of the table. Ollie turned his head to look at it. "Come *on*, Ollie," I muttered. "This right here is the yummiest mouse in the whole world, I swear. And it's all for you, you lucky bird." I jerked on the string, willing that mouse to look alive.

Ollie pounced in a wild flurry of feathers.

At dusk the next day, Travis and I towed Ollie in the wagon to Mr. Holloway's farm. It was time to let Ollie go. He was in the pink of health and ready to return to his life in the wild. He'd be lots happier, and I would be too. The only unhappy one was Travis, but then, he hadn't had to deal with the mice or the pellets or cleaning the cage.

Travis said, "Are you sure we can't keep him? He's so beautiful."

"Yes, he is beautiful, and no, we can't keep him."

"Maybe we could train him to eat other things."

"No." I didn't tell him that in my desperation I'd already tried chicken and corn and steak and peas and turnips and ham and even birdseed.

He'd shown not a whit of interest in
any of them.

"Maybe he'd eat—"

"No."

We met Mr. Holloway in the barn, where he was brushing his plow horse after a long day's work.

"I talked to my neighbors," he said, "and they've picked up their poison. So that there owl should be all right."

We went outside, and I put on the leather glove and pulled Ollie from the cage. Now that he was actually going, I felt a bit sad. I pulled the jess from his leg so that he wouldn't get it caught somewhere. I took a deep breath and threw my hand up into the air, expecting him to rush away, but he only flapped a few feet and settled on top of the barn.

"Go on, Ollie," said Travis. "Go and hunt."

"You call him Ollie?" said Mr. Holloway, squinting. "That owl's got a name?"

"Yes," I said, "but it doesn't mean anything. He won't come when he's called."

"Huh, too bad. That would be real handy."

Ollie picked up one foot and then the other and inspected his claws.

He looked out across Mr. Holloway's field and ruffled his feathers. Then he was gone, a blur, a ghost, flying silently before dropping like a white bullet into the field. A moment later he rose again, clutching a small object in his claws.

Ollie the Owl was gone. In his place was the *Tyto alba*, who'd caught a *Mus musculus*.